To Gerard

The author would like to acknowledge Robbii Albright for artwork assistance.
Additional artwork supplied by Frieda Premo.

PHILOMEL BOOKS

A division of Penguin Young Readers Group.
Published by The Penguin Group. Penguin Group (USA) Inc., 375 Hudson Street, New York, NY 10014, U.S.A.

The art for this book was made from all sorts of stuff. Some watercolor, some bits from old books, some gouache, a little amount of technology, some acrylic and even a bit of house paint. I think there is some oil paint on one page. But that might have been an accident.

Library of Congress Cataloging-in-Publication Data is available upon request.
ISBN 978-0-399-25452-9
10 9 8 7 6 5 4 3 2 1

OLIVER JEFFERS

The Heart and the BOTTLe

PHILOMEL BOOKS
An Imprint of Penguin Group (USA) Inc.

Once there was a girl, much like any other,

whose head was filled
with all the curiosities
of the world.

With thoughts of the stars.

With wonder at the sea.

She took delight in finding new things . . .

. . . until the day she found an empty chair.

Feeling unsure, the girl thought the best thing was to put her heart in a safe place.

Just for the time being.

So, she put it in a bottle and hung it around her neck.

And that seemed to fix things . . .

at first.

Although, in truth, nothing was the same.

She forgot about the stars . . .

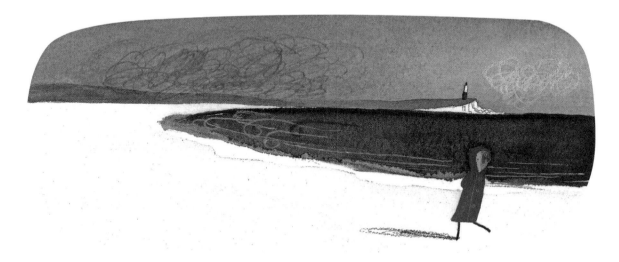

and stopped taking notice of the sea.

She was no longer filled
with all the curiosities of the
world and didn't take much
notice of anything . . .

other than how
heavy and awkward
the bottle had become.

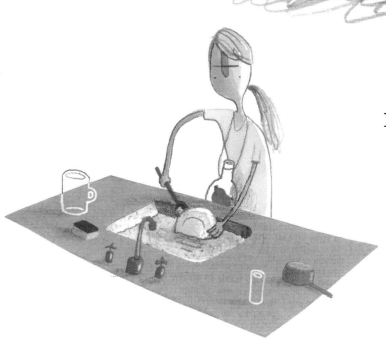

But at least her
heart was safe.

It might never have
occurred to the girl what to
do had she not met someone
smaller and still curious
about the world.

There was a time
when the girl would have
known how to answer her.

But not now.
Not without her heart.

And it was right
at that moment she decided
to get it back out of the bottle.

But she didn't know how.

She couldn't remember.

And nothing seemed to work.

The bottle couldn't be broken.

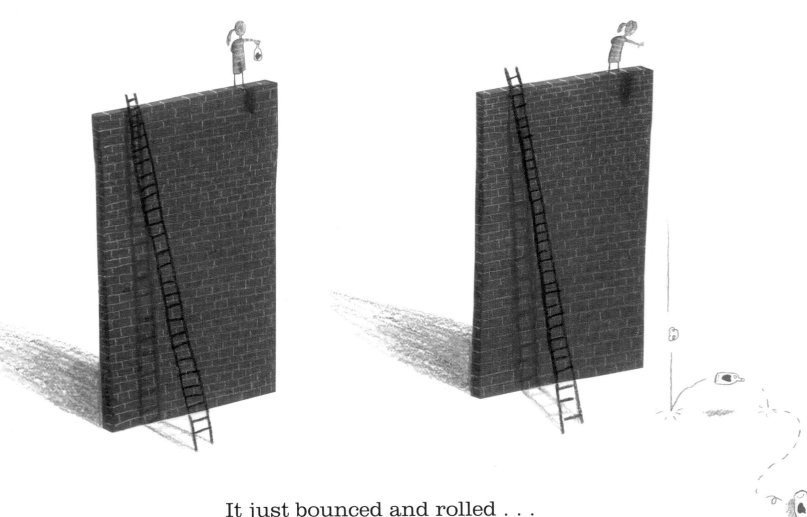

It just bounced and rolled . . .

right down to the sea.

But there, it occurred to someone
smaller and still curious about the world
that she might know a way.

And it just so happened . . .

she did.

The heart was put back where it came from.

And the chair wasn't so empty anymore.

But the bottle was.

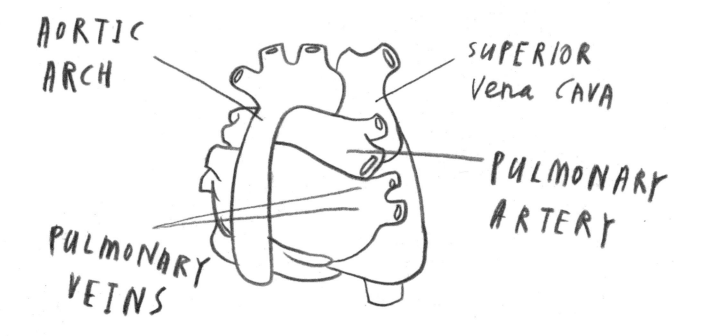

AORTIC
ARCH

SUPERIOR
Vena CAVA

PULMONARY
ARTERY

PULMONARY
VEINS

the
HEART AND VESSELS
(posterior view)